WILD EMM

CHILD OF ICELAND

Written by Ann Lane

&

Illustrated by Ben J. Greene

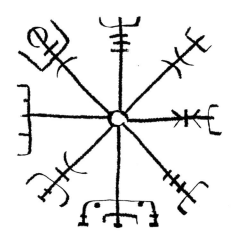

ISBN-13 : 978-1492703716

Dedications

To Jon and Margaret and all the people and horses
of Iceland who opened my eyes to the wonders of the
Land of Fire and Ice.

Doc, thank you for joining in on the round-ups and
exploring Iceland with me.

Alycin and Ben, thank you for advice and support
to make this book possible.

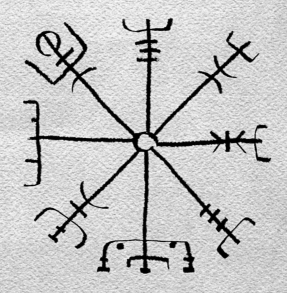

Emm lives in a land of fire and ice. Her home is Iceland, a country ringed by the sea and crossed with icy glaciers, and mountains that dip into lush green river valleys. Elves and trolls are thought to live in these magical mountains.

The elves dance on dewdrops sparkling on the rocks near waterfalls. Trolls, naughty little beings, hide in dark rocky areas, planning mischief.

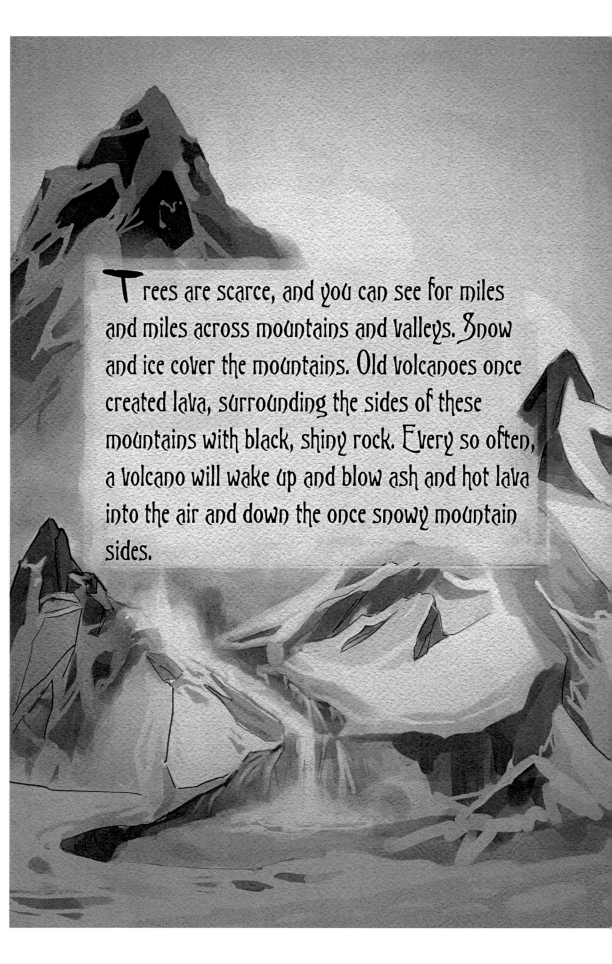

Trees are scarce, and you can see for miles and miles across mountains and valleys. Snow and ice cover the mountains. Old volcanoes once created lava, surrounding the sides of these mountains with black, shiny rock. Every so often, a volcano will wake up and blow ash and hot lava into the air and down the once snowy mountain sides.

Emm lives far away from the rumble
and threat of volcanoes. The mountains
ringing her farm are like friends. Their
furry, mossy crags look like balding, kindly
men, watching over her. Emm lives with her
brother, mom, and dad in a green valley.
Icelandic children call moms "Mamma," and
their fathers, "Pabbi."

Emm's grandmother, called Amma, knows that elves
live under the waterfalls, but Emm has never met any
of these small sprites. You see, Emm is a wild and loud
child, anxious to run instead of walk, and sing instead
of being quiet. Her best friend is the farm's border collie,
the Great One, and he loves to run and bark loudly
alongside her.

Amma told her that elves don't like a
lot of noise. Only whispers and patience
will coax them from their rocky homes.

Every fall, Emm, her brother, and Pabbi,
would ride over the mountains to the valley far
away to round up sheep and bring them home
to a barn for the cold winter months. Then,
every spring, Pabbi would drive the sheep and
their snowy lambs back over the mountain to
the green river valley. The horses were often
anxious, pawing and snorting after wintering
in the barn.

They would leap and run while Emm rode in
front of the saddle with her Pabbi. Her Pabbi would cry
out, "Whoa, slow down!" while Emm would secretly cry,
"Faster, go faster!" The horses would carry them over
beautiful rocky mountains, through difficult and cold
rivers, until they saw the wild sheep darting in and out of
crevices, like white cotton balls blown by the wind. Then
the fun would begin, with the Great One silently finding
the hidden sheep, while Emm tried her best to catch the
snowy lambs to deliver to Pabbi.

Emm would race up the mountain sides on foot, outrunning the snowy lambs and wide-eyed ewes. On horseback, her brother could never outrun her. Her Mamma and Amma told her that one day, if she continued to be so wild, she would turn into a wild Icelandic horse. Emm knew that this must be a joke, and would laugh, toss her head, and race up another mountain side.

One summer morning, Pabbi said it was time
to drive the sheep back over the mountain and
into the next valley so they could eat fresh
grass with their new lambs. This was Emm's
favorite task, as Pabbi's horse, she, and
the Great One could run up the mountain alone.

That day, dark clouds blew cold wind around the sheep's feet and legs. Frightened and chilled, the sheep went wild. Up and down the mountain they flew, bucking and bleating. Emm's Pabbi said, "Now, Emm, you and the Great One, go and turn the sheep back down the mountain."

Emm ran up and up, farther than she had ever traveled before. At first, she could hear her brother and Pabbi calling, "Emm, please come back!" but she continued to run up and up until the land touched the clouds. Finally, Emm could hear only the distant bleat of a lone wild sheep. "I will catch that sheep," she said to herself, twisting through the brush. By now, the dog had turned back to his master's call, but Emm hadn't noticed.

As she ran, she felt her steps getting lighter and faster, until climbing big rocks and jumping streams was easy. She noticed her bangs had grown longer, and she tossed her head to keep them out of her eyes. She could see much farther now, and felt much taller. Suddenly, after jumping over a crevasse, she saw a wild sheep standing in front of her, drinking from a stream. It didn't run when she stomped her feet, and when she yelled at it only a funny whinny came out of her mouth. Looking into the stream, Emm saw a blonde horse staring back at her.

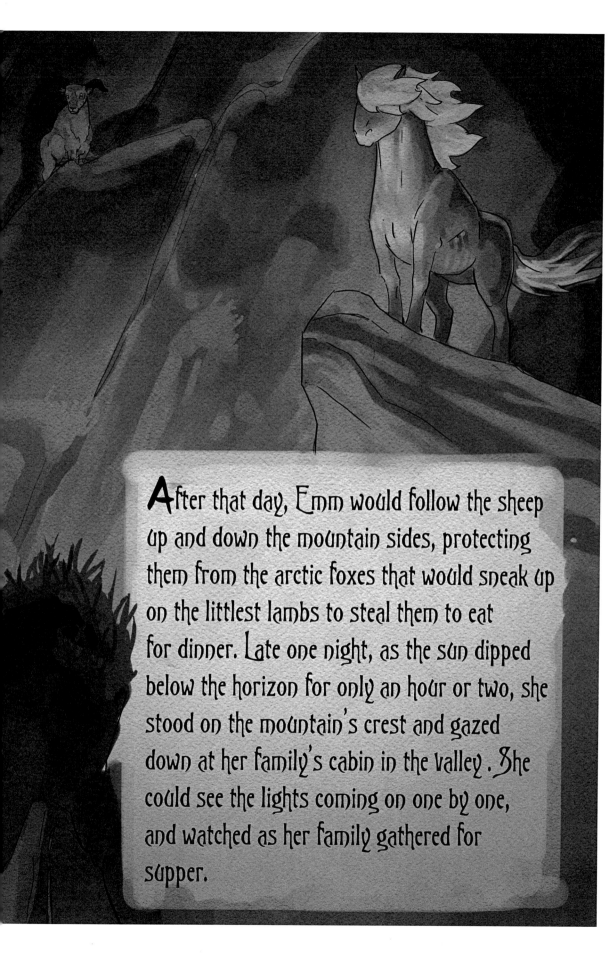

After that day, Emm would follow the sheep up and down the mountain sides, protecting them from the arctic foxes that would sneak up on the littlest lambs to steal them to eat for dinner. Late one night, as the sun dipped below the horizon for only an hour or two, she stood on the mountain's crest and gazed down at her family's cabin in the valley. She could see the lights coming on one by one, and watched as her family gathered for supper.

One silent tear fell from her eye, and Emm whispered, "I want to go home." A small rustle stirred at her feet. She glanced down and saw a small person sitting in the moss. An elf! He looked at her kindly and he could see the small girl inside the wild horse. He winked at her and asked her to follow him. She cautiously walked down the darkening path, being careful to not step on the little sprite.

She followed the elf into a glistening cave, a secret spot tucked away behind a rushing waterfall. The cave was lined with soft moss, and Emm lay down, realizing how tired she was.

"Now, what seems to be your problem?" the kindly elf asked.

"I am really a girl," wailed Emm. "But I turned into a horse because I always raced too fast and ran away so often."

"No," said the elf, shaking his bearded face. "You were bewitched by Gryla, a jealous, naughty troll who lives in the rocks on the mountain top. She always wanted to run and play like you, but she wasn't brave. She hid away in her cave and never played as a child. Now she is old and sad. She wants to take the fun away from children."

And with that said, the elf waved his funny long arms and turned Emm back into a girl. Next to her a swirling cloud of sparkling dust wove its way into the shape of a silver horse.

"This is Wind Racer," said the elf. "Should you ever again feel like running and running, just get on her and she will take you up, but most importantly, take you down the mountains safely to your home."

Emm became friends with the fleet-footed silver horse. Emm now races over the mountains on Racer and helps round up sheep. She loves to run and ride, but now she makes sure she answers when her parents call her and she is never late for supper.

Ann Lane, a nurse practitioner , has over 20 years experience coaching parents and children with special needs. She enjoys telling them stories that fire their imagination and sense of wonder. International horseback riding holidays and travel inspire her own sense of adventure. Ann lives on a farm near High Springs, Florida with her husband and a variety of critters, including a llama named Mike.

Ann is currently working on several sequels narrating Wild Emm's adventures.

Ben is an art director and concept artist in the video game industry. He curently lives in Gainesville, FL with his wife and four children.

Ben's wife comes from a long and rich line of Icelanders. He has been deeply steeped in the people and culture and has greatly enjoyed having the chance to participate in the Wild Emm story.

Made in the USA
Middletown, DE
14 June 2016